# THE PERILS

# *of*

# PIERRE

## Book 1
### *Gold Fever*

by

**Ian Janssen**

**WEE CREEK PRESS**

www.weecreekpress.com

Published by
WEE CREEK PRESS
www.weecreekpress.com
An Imprint of
WHISKEY CREEK PRESS
PO Box 51052
Casper, WY 82605-1052
www.whiskeycreekpress.com

Ebook ISBN: 978-1-61160-900-4
Print ISBN: 978-1-61160-594-5

**Cover Artist and Illustrator: Susan Ruby K**
**Editor: Jan Janssen**
**Line Editor: Steve Womack**
**Interior Design: Jim Brown**
**Printed in the United States of America**

# DEDICATION

I would like to dedicate this book to my late mother, Elizabeth Janssen, who always said I had an active imagination.

# Chapter 1

Deep in the northern forest there lived two odd friends, who were always seeking new adventures together. Polly the Crow would fly high over the forest looking for something that she and her friend, Pierre the Fox, could investigate.

Today, Polly was flying over the north ridge of Loon Lake when she spotted something shiny in the crack of the rock. She flew to the ground to investigate and discovered a gold chain. It was stuck between the rock and an old dried up poplar tree.

She grabbed the chain in her beak and yanked at it, but the chain would not budge. She soon realized that she would need help to get the chain, so she quickly flew off, searching for her friend Pierre the Fox.

First, she searched along the highway, as she knew Pierre liked to spend time there, but he was nowhere to be seen.

Next, Polly searched along the south shore of Loon Lake and the creek emptying out of the lake. This was a special area for Pierre, for this was the area where he was born. Again, Pierre was nowhere to be found.

Polly was getting worried. Pierre was *never* this hard to find. After all, he was a bright red colour, and he was easy to spot against the green forest.

Polly continued to circle around, looking for Pierre. She was making her circles wider and wider, so she could check further out for Pierre.

Finally, she spotted some red near the old tree nursery. It was Pierre! Polly flew down and landed beside her fox friend. "Pierre," she said. "I have been looking all over for you! What are you doing way down here in the old tree nursery?"

"I was exploring around the old copper mine on the south shore of Loon Lake, then I just wandered further and further, and here I am!" said Pierre.

"But Pierre, don't you know you can get lost that way? You should let someone know where you are, and where you intend to go," scolded Polly.

Pierre was nowhere to be found.

"Well, I'm not *that* far away, am I?" asked Pierre. "After all, you found me didn't you?"

"Yes, I did. This time!" said Polly. "But only because I was looking for you to go on an adventure with me."

"What kind of adventure, huh?" Pierre sounded excited.

"Well, I was doing some exploring of my own on the ridge on the north side of Loon Lake and I spotted something shiny! I went down to see what it was and it was a gold chain!"

Pierre cocked his head at Polly. "So, where is it?"

"It is still where I found it because it is stuck between a rock and an old poplar tree. I'm not strong enough to get it out. That is why I came looking for you."

"Cool! Let's go get it!" declared Pierre.

Polly shook her head. "No. It's going to get dark soon and I don't fly in the dark. Let's get it in the morning. We'll meet at the green cabin on the north shore of Loon Lake, and I can direct you from the air"

"Well, I'm not that far away, am I? After all, you found me didn't you?"

"Okay, in the morning it is," Pierre agreed.

That night, all Pierre could think about was going to look for the gold chain. After all, *he* could see perfectly in the dark. It should be easy for him to find! So, he set out on his own to look for the chain Polly told him about.

In no time at all he was on the north ridge. Well, the north ridge runs for miles and miles. Before long he was up at T Lake, far away from his home, and he *still* hadn't found the chain.

He searched and searched, but it was quickly becoming daylight. Pierre thought he should go home and meet up with Polly. But when he turned around to head back, he realized that he could not see T Lake. He did not know where he was!

Was he lost? No! He couldn't be! After all, he was a fox, and foxes are smart and cunning! But…he was not sure what direction to take to reach the green cabin on Loon Lake.

*Oh!* he thought. *What am I going to do? Polly warned me about wandering off alone, and not letting anyone know where I was going.*

Was he lost?No! He couldn't be! After all, he was a fox.

Pierre sat down and thought about how he was going to find his way back.

While sitting there, thinking, he was also staring at the ground and he saw something shiny sticking out of a crack in the rock. He started digging at it and pulled out a gold chain.

Polly must have been wrong about where she saw the gold chain! He kept digging and found more treasure! There was a gold watch, a gold ring and lots of other shiny jewelry! Wow!

Pierre started digging and pulled out a gold chain!

# CHAPTER 2

But Pierre still had a problem…how was he going to find Polly and tell her of his discovery? There was no way he could carry *all* the treasure that he discovered. He had to find a way to mark the spot. Then Polly could find it from the air, and tell him how to get back here.

But wait, he didn't know where he *was*, so how was he going to find Polly and tell her how to get here?

Pierre was stumped. What was he going to do? Again he sat down to try and solve this problem.

*I've got it!* thought Pierre. *Polly found me the last time when I was in the old tree nursery, so when I don't show up at the green cabin, she will start to search for me again.*

Now Pierre was happy. He would soon be found by Polly. He was sure of it!

Pierre was very shy around strangers.

*But wait,* thought Pierre again. *Will Polly even think about looking for me in this direction? And how will she see me in this thick forest? I have to find a clearing, so she can easily spot my red coat.*

So, Pierre quickly set out to find a clearing.

Pierre got further and further away from his treasure site and still hadn't found a good clearing. And now he could not find his way back to his treasure!

*What am I going to do now?* thought Pierre.

He sat down and looked for a path or a tree that seemed familiar.

While he was sitting there he saw a black squirrel. It was perched on an old log nearby, watching him.

"My name is Pierre," said the fox. "I am from the south shore of Loon Lake, and I am lost. Could you help me find my way back?" It was hard for Pierre to talk to the squirrel, because his only friend was Polly the Crow. He was very shy around strangers.

The squirrel said his name was Fred, and that he would be glad to help Pierre. He asked what he could do.

"I could climb to the top
of the highest tree!"

Pierre was new at being lost, so was not sure what Fred the squirrel *could* do.

"I could climb to the top of the highest tree and see if I can spot Loon Lake for you," said Fred. "Then I could point you in the right direction."

This sounded great to Pierre, so Fred did just that. He climbed the highest tree he could find and looked all around. At last he saw Loon Lake! He told Pierre which way he had to go.

Before Pierre set out home, he thanked Fred the Squirrel. Then he asked him if he would like to join him and Polly the Crow in a treasure hunt on the ridge north of Loon Lake. Fred shook his head. "No, thank you," he said. "I have to stay here. My family is here, and I like to be near them."

Meanwhile, Polly had already arrived at the green cabin and did not find Pierre there. She thought he must have gone on without her. Pierre could be so impatient! She started flying around in circles looking for her good friend.

A short time later, Fred the Squirrel saw a dark bird flying in ever widening circles around Loon Lake. He

"That was a lot of work getting all of the treasure here!"

scampered from branch to branch, high in the trees, and signaled the bird with a loud chirping sound. He was *sure* this must be Pierre's friend, Polly the Crow!

Soon, Polly saw the squirrel trying to get her attention and she flew over to investigate.

Polly and Pierre were finally reunited, and she got to meet Pierre's new friend, Fred the Squirrel.

Pierre was quick to tell Polly about his adventures, the new treasure that he found, how he met Fred the Squirrel, and how Fred helped him to be found by Polly.

With the help of Fred, Polly and Pierre located the treasure that Pierre had found. They said their goodbyes to Fred, quickly gathered up the treasure and headed for the green cabin on the north shore of Loon Lake.

After depositing their treasure on the dock, Polly and Pierre decided they still had time to go up on the north ridge to find the shiny gold chain that Polly had seen. Soon, with the help of Pierre, they got the chain loose from the rock and the old poplar tree.

They found even more treasure with the gold chain, so

The boys jumped up and down in excitement. "Look what we found!"

they gathered it up too and took it to the dock at the green cabin.

Once they got all of the treasure together on the dock, Pierre said to Polly, "That was a *lot* of work getting all of the treasure here!" Polly agreed. She was tired after all their adventures!

Night was falling, so they agreed to leave their treasure on the dock. Pierre would watch over it during the night.

First thing the next morning, just as Pierre was waking up, he heard a commotion and hurried into the brush to hide. The owners had come to their cabin for the weekend!

Two young boys, Ehren and Keenan—who are cousins—ran to the lake, while their parents unloaded the cars. Pierre watched as they quickly spotted the treasure on the dock, that he and Polly had worked so hard to collect.

The boys jumped up and down in excitement. Wow! Look at all the shiny treasure just lying there waiting for them!

Both boys yelled to their Dads. "Look what we found!"

# ABOUT THE AUTHOR

My name is Ian Janssen from Elliot Lake, Ontario. I am a retired police officer who enjoys spending time at the cottage with my four grandchildren. I decided to write these stories for them, and ultimately, to share them with others.

# ABOUT THE ILLUSTRATOR

Susan Ruby K is a freelance artist residing in Northern Ontario, Canada. Yuneekpix.com

*For your reading pleasure, we invite you to
visit our web bookstore*

An Imprint of Whiskey Creek Press

**WEE CREEK PRESS**

**www.weecreekpress.com**

CPSIA information can be obtained
at www.ICGtesting.com
Printed in the USA
LVIC01n0810040314
375695LV00002B/2